Turtle's *Adventure*
in Alphabet Town

written and illustrated
by Janet McDonnell

created by Wing Park Publishers

CHILDRENS PRESS ®
CHICAGO

Library of Congress Cataloging-in-Publication Data

McDonnell, Janet, 1962-
　　Turtle's adventure in Alphabet Town / written and illustrated by
　Janet McDonnell.
　　　　p.　　cm. — (Read around Alphabet Town)
　　Summary: Turtle takes a trip to visit his friend Tiger in an
　adventure filled with "t" words.
　　ISBN 0-516-05420-1
　　[1. Turtles—Fiction.　2. Travel—Fiction.　3. Alphabet.]　I.
　Title.　II. Series.
　PZ7.M1547Tu　1992
　[E]—dc 20　　　　　　　　　　　　　　　　　92-2984
　　　　　　　　　　　　　　　　　　　　　　　　　CIP
　　　　　　　　　　　　　　　　　　　　　　　　　AC

Turtle's *Adventure*
in Alphabet Town

You are now entering Alphabet Town,
With houses from "A" to "Z."
I'm going on a "T" adventure today,
So come along with me.

This is the "T" house of Alphabet
Town. Turtle lives here.

Turtle likes "t" things. He has
lots of them in his house.

Turtle likes to play with his toys.

And he likes to play tag.

Most of all, Turtle likes to take trips. One day, Turtle's

telephone

rang.

It was Turtle's friend,

Tiger.

"Would you like to come to my town?" asked Tiger. "We will have fun together!"

"Terrific!" said Turtle. "I love to take trips."

"Come tomorrow at two o'clock," said Tiger. "And be on time."

The next day, Turtle filled the

tub.

He took a bath.

He brushed his teeth. Then he put on his best

tie.

Tick, tock, went the clock. "Time
to go," said Turtle.

Turtle called a

"Take me to Tiger's house," said
Turtle.

The taxi drove along for ten miles.
But then, POW! The taxi ran over a
tack.

"A flat

tire!"

said Turtle. "This is terrible.
What will I do?"

Just then, along came his friend
Toad in a

truck.

"Hop in," said Toad. "I will
take you to Tiger's house."

19

Turtle was very happy. The truck drove along for twenty miles. Soon it came to a

tunnel.

The truck drove into the tunnel.
But then, CRUNCH!

"Oh, no!" said Toad. "My truck is too tall for this tunnel. It is stuck."
"This is terrible," said Turtle.
"What will I do?"

Just then, he heard a TOOT,
TOOT!

It was the whistle of a

train.

TOOT! TOOT!

TICKETS

"I will take the train!" said Turtle.

He bought a ticket. Then he
climbed onto the train.

The train took Turtle down the
tracks . . .

all the way to Tiger's town. When
Turtle got there, he called Tiger
on the telephone.

"I am sorry I am late," said
Turtle. "I took a taxi, a truck,
and a train to get here."

"But, Turtle," said Tiger, "you are right on time!" And he was.

MORE FUN WITH TURTLE

What's in a Name?

In my "t" adventure, you read many "t" words. My name begins with a "T." Many of my friends' names begin with "T" too. Here are a few.

Timothy

Tina

Terry

Tamica

Tanya

Tom

Tricia

Ted

Do you know other names that start with "T"?

Does your name start with "T"?

Turtle's Word Hunt

I like to hunt for "t" words. Can you help me find the words on this page that begin with "t"? How many are there? Can you read them?

bat

turkey

mittens

clown

mountain

shirt

top

Can you find any words with "t" in the middle?
Can you find any with "t" at the end?
Can you find a word with no "t"?

Turtle's Favorite Things

"T" is my favorite letter. I love "t" things. Can you guess why? You can find some of my favorite "t" things in my house on page 7. How many "t" things can you find there? Can you think of more "t" things?

Now you make up a "t" adventure.